One Way or Another

So it happened. A cold splash into the water, a gritting of teeth, a strong stroke to beyond the waves that broke forever, near the shore.

"It's too f–ing cold," Randy said to himself, "but so be it."

He slowed the pace, he floated awhile, he looked up to the blue, very blue, sky above.

"Thank God," he said aloud. "Alone, finally.

"Now don't drown out here."

He floated until he sank too much, he swam toward the shore. "A meal," he told himself. "Like my wife used to make." He'd never known meals like that again (after she left him). He toweled dry, thinking: "But just as long as it's *close*" – chili and beans, lettuce on the side, a turkey leg if he was especially hungry. Like this day.

The house wasn't very big, but big enough for Randy. His father'd left it to him and he kept it after the divorce, his wife saying, "Who needs that shit? I want money!"

Okay, she had her own business.

He strode up the steps from the beach, he flipped on a light, he pulled open the screen door, entered. Jasmine had gone for the day. She worked once a week, this was a day she'd worked – cleaning, doing laundry, dishes, watering the few patio plants, making that bed.

Randy drank a half glassful of water, changed his trunks for soft sleepwear. No shower. Screw it.

He had the chili in the fridge, and a salad he tossed together, a turkey leg he cut away from the half-turkey on the lower shelf of the fridge, a bottle of beer, a UFO documentary on T.V. – a respite from the news programs Randy often watched.

The evening wore on. The phone rang but he didn't answer.

Nightmares, later. A cold sweat. The clock read: 1:30. And a knock on the front door, the alley door. Randy grunted and padded to the front, away from the beach entrance, saw through the peephole it was Sophia, the black woman he'd dated infrequently. Wow.

Upon opening his door to her she said, "Oh, hell, I know it's late. Let me in?"

"Sure."

Sophia entered, her brown eyes sheepish. "Sorry! I've gotten kicked out for the night." She held an overnight bag.

Randy's jaw dropped; she laughed. "Tried calling you, but I know how you don't like to answer your phone." She wandered in. "Hope you're alone!" she fairly shouted, looking the place over.

"I usually am."

"I know."

A drink or two, a conversation, a nodding Randy. 2:00 am.

"Put me on the couch," Sophia suggested finally.

"Fine."

Her new husband had hit her, had screamed at her, had made her leave, at least for one night. That was her story; Randy was not inclined to disbelieve her.

In the morning she showered and insisted on preparing breakfast. Randy ran a mile in the sand and returned, not troubled at leaving her alone in his house – not much to steal there, anyway. She had always been trustworthy, but for lying occasionally.

"Gotta get away from him," he told her while they ate. "Really."

"Yes, I know. I will."

She left not too long after breakfast, to go get stuff from the house she'd lived in for just three months. Her husband would (hopefully) be at work – Sophia could pack and head for her mother in Pasadena.

Special circumstances now, he informed himself, after she'd gone. "A bad guy. If he thinks I'm the one responsible for her leaving him, could be dangerous." So Randy pulled out his two pistols, loaded them, put one in a drawer in the bedroom and one in his desk in the living room/study/library.

As people said, "Safety first."

Domestic problems! Best to not get involved. Yet, he'd told her to leave the guy. Randy sat on his deck the next day, wondering if Sophia would phone. He watched the surf, he drank a beer, he had a small cigar.

If she called he'd have to play it smart, expressing a wish to remain out of this mess. She'd argue, maybe, but he had to inform her that a domestic dispute wasn't a concern of his; he'd rather avoid it. She may or may not understand. She probably would, although not liking it.

If she cried, could he resist? Keep away? But of course he *had* to. He determined to resist the impulse to help her, if she cried on the phone. Did he want to get killed by an enraged husband? Not much.

Sundays meant it was more crowded on the beach. Families, etc.

He stayed indoors. Solitary sort of person, he was. Watching T.V. and reading and writing. There was the Presidential election coming up in a very few months. Randy wasn't sure who he'd vote for – Carter or Reagan. Carter was not as strong and confident as he had been in '76. Reagan had some new kind of ideas: tax cuts, etc. The economy was slipping. Let a new guy in to fix it? But Randy thought Reagan was phony, pretending to be such a fine person. Perhaps he was, but who knew? But Randy felt it was an act, that in fact Reagan was mean inside. He saw quick glimpses of it on the news. At least he believed so.

No calls from Sophia. Good.

On Monday morning, he went for a swim. Then a shower, then had orange juice, toast, fried eggs, a couple of cups of coffee. He didn't turn on the T.V. or the radio. He still dreaded a call from Sophia. At ten his agent called, no word from the publisher about their last submission. Since Randy's one successful novel, in 1975, the material he'd submitted was not exciting any big reaction.

His "deal" was weak: if the publisher liked a manuscript Randy produced, the publisher could go with it; if he didn't, he wouldn't. It was a ten year contract. After that, whatever Randy wrote could be sent to anyone – if his agent agreed. The first book he'd written, Randy self-published – at a cost – and it didn't sell. In fact, he could barely find bookstores to carry it. *But* then he got the publishing contract (weak as it was) and *that* next book sold 89,000 copies. A moderate success. Very few books sold millions, contrary to common perception.

So Randy had kept writing.

His next one would be his best, he determined. It had more action in it. Readers liked action. A thoughtful, meandering story didn't appeal to readers these days. Not generally, at least.

But Randy was a thoughtful guy. One of the things his ex-wife had complained about. "You're just, just, *sitting* there! What's wrong with you?"

He couldn't explain. If only he'd come up with a simple answer, she might have understood. "I'm thinking."

Except she'd have asked: about what? And he'd have had a hard time responding, but that was better than saying nothing, which is what he did do. He *was* thinking, sitting there, but…for some reason he wasn't able to verbalize it. He'd just weathered the criticism (as usual). And she would be disgusted every time it happened.

So the marriage fell apart.

Fell apart, bit by bit.

Not that that mattered. Randy had fairly lost all attraction toward her after a few years of her criticisms. It wasn't that his eye was wandering. It was more as if the passion had left the partnership. And she felt the same lack in regard to him.

So he sat on the deck chair and got some sun – not that he needed it, for he already had a bronze-like tan. Sophia had chided him how White folks try to get brown, yet many dislike brown (and Black) people. For sure he had no clever comeback for that, being as it was the truth. Not that she thought he himself was racist.

His lunch was chicken and rice and beans and some lettuce.

He napped and then wrote in his novel. Action! Action! the Muse implored him. Randy had been a news writer for his college paper, for a semester, and quit because the pace was beyond him – he was so slow in whatever he did! But he recalled the campus news *had* contained: a fistfight, a death by heart attack, and a drunk driver smashing through the front door of his dormitory. That was action, was it not? All he need do is provide a back story for the drunk, and a tragic death of a bystander, and...and...he tossed his pencil on the notebook before him. "Hell," he exclaimed. "There's nowhere to take the story. My mind's a blank!"

"A bystander? Hit by the drunk driver? That could be all right, and following the lives of the bystander's family and loved ones…"

But oddly, it bored him. It was nearly a formula...nay, it *was* a formula. Randy wanted to write something more interesting. At least to him. But what?

The neighbors next door were having a party that night. Of course he wasn't invited, having barely said a word to them in the six months after they'd moved in. "Shucks! I must make an effort, become more sociable. Why not?"

The T.V. entertained him, as the noise from next door polluted his house. Could write about some bad neighbors, he thought, having a drug party, a conflict, a bunch of arguments, a murder...yeah.

Little did he know.

He awoke with the loud hollering, louder than the festive sounds, music, ext door. He rose and peeked out his side window. Across the way, on a small but adequate balcony, level with his second floor bedroom, were a man and a woman struggling.

"I'll kill you," the man said, in a screeching tone.

"Try that, you son of a bitch!" the middle-aged woman yelled. They struggled a bit more, hands gripping the other wildly, and a short, shave-headed, stocky man came into view, also hollering, "Enough, enough!"

"No, just try that!" the woman repeated, as the bigger man froze, suddenly, seeing the stocky one approaching.

"Never you mind, I'll deal with you another time," the man screeched, and released his grip on her shoulders. She smacked him on the side of his face, and the shaved-head man yanked her away. "Calm yourself, Beverly."

"To hell with you both," she said, pulling free, and ran from the balcony.

Randy stared in wonder, but now the two men stood as quiet as statues. He backed away from the window lest either man turn their head and possibly spot him.

What an event! he remarked to himself, silently, as he made his way deeper into his bedroom.

Sleep came fitfully, mainly in spite of the music next door, but a crying (wailing, actually) from that upper floor, inside of the balcony, kept him awake. And a "shot" woke him fully, but he wasn't actually positive it was a gunshot. A grunt, discernible in the silence, followed. Randy rose to his elbows. Then a glass broke, he thought, but that sound was faint, coming also from within the house. A shot, a grunt, a breaking glass – what did it mean?

Then, lying in bed, Randy began to drowse. But sleep eluded him. A siren came from further away. Oh God, he thought. A police siren? He rose as he heard it at the front of the house, heard it shut off, and car doors slam.

He waited but no discernible sounds came to his ears. Apparently the police had been summoned, but why, he couldn't know. Perhaps the neighbor on the other side was fed up with the noise, or a gun *had* indeed been fired, and someone injured, or worse.

The following morning brought two uniformed city employees to his door on the alley. They questioned him as to what he'd heard, perchance, during the night. He told them. He even included the activity on the patio. Why not? It was illegal to lie to cops, wasn't it? To leave out that event would be a lie, once when they asked could he recall anything other than music and voices, and a sound like a shot, if he said "Nothing else," they *could* come back with the man having said Randy saw, and no doubt heard, the argument. Then what?

The policemen gave him precious little information on their side.

"Was anyone wounded?" he asked them.

"We can't reveal that," he was told.

Later Randy realized he'd forgotten to mention the sound of a grunt and then the sound of a breaking glass (after the sound of a gun). "Oh well," he remarked to himself. "What's the difference? If they come again, I'll tell them."

But what had happened during that night? He wanted to go next door and ask. But should he? Perhaps he would be rebuffed, and then, embarrassed. A more aggressive person than *he* would march over and demand information. After all, the cops had questioned him – involved him, so to speak. But Randy was a recluse, a weak person, actually, in societal actions.

Better to keep his mouth shut, to see what occurred – if anything.

Nothing did, other than two more visits by police next door. No one, though, came near his abode. It occurred to Randy that a coroner's vehicle *could* have picked up a body that first night – while he was asleep. Dramatic? Yes. His mind worked like that.

He ran on the beach, he even approached the house in question, looking up inside as best he could. He saw no one. There was a good excuse for curiosity, especially him having been questioned by authorities, but there was no confrontation by his neighbors.

So, then he sat and wrote in his book for awhile. He drank a beer afterward, felt a discomfort that was unusual for him. He *had* to find out what occurred that night. The newspaper revealed nothing. Should he call the police? Randy decided to, yet the actual doing of it gave him pause. Would the police think him guilty of...something or other? Not knowing the circumstances kept him from deciding if he was free from suspicion. Finally, he called and talked his way to a sergeant who was handling "the incident" at such-and-such an address, and such-and-such a date.

"Really, all I'd like to know is what occurred. After all, I live in the next house."

"Sure, understandable. I've seen the report of your interview."

"Yes?" Randy said, judiciously.

"What I can tell you is there was a shooting, and the victim passed away after being transported to the ER that night."

"Well, wow! Who was it?"

"A guest at the gathering that evening. The party."

"Who shot him?"

"It was a she, a young woman. The victim. Who shot her must remain confidential at present. Do you have any more information? In addition to your previous statement?"

Randy ignored that. "So you know who did the shooting, the killing?"

"Yes."

"Why not tell me? Was it one of the folks I saw on the balcony, fighting?"

"Sir, I repeat,l that must remain confidential at present."

"Okay. I'm a nobody, of course, but I did hear a sound, a loud exhale, or a grunt, after the sound of the shot."

That information apparently meant little to the policeman.

"And a glass breaking. Must have been a large one, for me to hear it from inside, you know."

"Yes. Anything else?"

"Not that I remember."

"Well, it's appreciated, Mr. Whynn."

"Okay," Randy hung up, dissatisfied.

So much for that. All he could do now was watch newspapers, perhaps ask a question if an inhabitant of the neighboring house became available, and bide his time. Surely it all was intriguing, but not, so much, any of his business.

Time passed. Several weeks. He continued work on his novel. He ate beef and salad and vegetables and ran on the beach at low tide. He even spoke with a man on the patio of the house, exchanging greetings and pleasantries, but discovered nothing because it was harder to broach the subject, for him, than he'd anticipated. *Next* time, he told himself. The man said his name was Prescott Irwin. Randy got that much, anyway.

Funny, anticipating things. He'd done it all his life, imagining first how something would go, and then seeing how close his idea turned out to be, in reality. A friend of his, perhaps two years ago, who'd gotten deep in to the current fad of the time "e.s.t." (it was called) had told him flat out: "Don't anticipate!" That must've been one of the precepts of the training, or whatever, that Erhard, the founder of "e.s.t." had formulated. But since

Randy didn't care for the way his friend was behaving, had come under the influence of the Erhard "training," Randy shied away from the advice.

Nevertheless, the questioning Randy had envisioned himself doing when meeting up with an inhabitant of that house didn't materialize. He was reluctant, and now, a bit ashamed of himself. Why? Did he think he'd get shot, too? Maybe.

The sun slanted down pleasantly on the porch. A few children played in the surf, a few adults sat on the sand, keeping an eye on them. Randy dozed, his housekeeper worked, his phone didn't ring. A fine pleasant day, so far. But he was troubled, about what he knew not. The book was going well, if slowly, as usual. But what bothered him? He stared at the sea. He thought, "One of these days life will make sense." He was certain of that.

Since childhood he had felt life confusing, and plain perplexing, really. His parents had divorced, he'd gone in the Army, he'd worked as a clerk in a convenience store, he'd inherited a goodly sum when his father died (in a boating accident), and he'd married. Yet all along, he felt pushed and pulled as if by a strange tempest. He'd struggled to enjoy life, but always that mysteriously eluded him – the happiness he sought.

But life was not without reward for hard work: success of a sort in his writing, joy of a sort in his marriage, fun of a sort with Sophia. But all the time a bizarre unpleasantness prevailed. Real happiness eluded him. Why? He didn't know. An unfulfilled dream? An unfulfilled desire? He wanted more than what he had. Perhaps that explained why aspects of his life worked for a time, but then failed – he was always vaguely dissatisfied, so he persisted in looking beyond his current circumstances, refusing to settle for what he had. Even the beach was beginning to bore him. That was a shock. Luckily he didn't have a dog or a cat, even. They'd be boring him now, also.

Was he a prisoner of his own making?

The phone rang. He answered and discovered it was Sophia, pleading for a bed, a meal, a comfortable place to hide from her husband.

"Oh, no!" Randy exclaimed. "What happened?"

"Please, I'll tell you, but do say I may spend the evening, won't you?"

And against his better judgment, Randy acquiesced.

She arrived all "aflutter," as they say, running into his arms. By the time they drank, and ate, and he comforted her, Sophia explained she'd returned to her husband and he'd beaten her, of course, after a brief time of uneasy truce.

Randy grimaced, he frowned, he scowled, he smiled (to improve her spirits). She slept in his bed, he held her, he let her touch him, and one thing led to another.

By morning they were bonded, as in times past, but the day brought reckoning. Brad called. They argued on the phone while Randy paced, and she left abruptly.

"So much for that," he told himself. If she kills Brad, or he kills her, what could he do to prevent it? That question appeared rhetorical, but Randy spent an hour pondering and regretting participating in adultery.

He came up with nothing very reasonable: take her in, try and shoot him if he arrived, half-crazed and frantic? Well, now, hardly practical, if Brad was armed.

Randy thrust the problem from his mind, not with ease, but at last, successfully. He also reminded himself he hadn't been to a firing range for target practice in a decade.

He ran on the beach again, he scanned the neighbors' house but saw no activity. The determination to uncover the details of that wild night still occupied him.

The hostage crisis continued in Iran. When would it be over?

He shopped for groceries, although Jasmine offered to do it. He needed the excuse to mingle with others, to drive, to watch people. A writer needs to observe life, does he not? He went to a bookstore looking for a new book. An old one, however, struck his fancy. Solzhenitsyn's "In the First Circle." Censored, it was, but still, he realized while reading it, powerful. What the people had gone through! American life was much easier than life in the Soviet Union.

He watched the news, the Presidential contest, the local news. The summer was waning, like a beautiful evening moon.

"Murder! Help me!" was the loud call from next door. But Randy was on the beach, near a house two places over from his, the white house beside the notorious one (next to his). He was merely on a walk, on the sand, and a lonely figure, an old pale lady, emerged on the white house's deck.

"What's that?" she asked, looking down at him.

"I have no idea, but it sounds serious," he informed the lady.

As she continued to stare at him he walked quickly to the notorious house, climbed the outside staircase, and viewed that patio. "Help!" came a new yell, in the same voice.

"What's the matter?"

Silence. He advanced onto the patio, seeing a woman face down backwards through an open door. A man then sprang out of the doorway, charging at her, and Randy himself sprang forward.

"Hold on there, pardner," he exclaimed, raising his hands as the man neared the prone woman.

Randy was at first brushed aside, but establishing a grip on the man's arm, wrenched it firmly, stopping the man's advance.

The woman rolled around on the deck, moaning. Randy pulled the man further away; the man made a noise like a growl, and tried to free his arm by pushing with his free hand, but Randy's fierce determination was too much for him to overcome, so he sputtered stupidly, "Stop it!" Still Randy held on, expecting a punch but none came. The man gave up struggling.

It turned out they were married, and urged Randy to go away, to mind his own business.

Of course back in his own dwelling he thought of Sophie – was she going through much the same?

But in spite of the warning, Randy went to the *next* house over and spoke with the old lady. She sat him on a couch inside, she herself plopping down in a wheelchair.

"So you kept the boy from murdering her?" A smile played across her lips.

"It's possible," he replied.

"I didn't call the police, but almost...wouldn't be the first time."

"Are you aware there was a shooting over there last month?"

"Yes," she said, no smile now visible. "A friend of theirs was killed, so the police told me."

"I heard the shot. I saw an argument on a balcony on my side of that house. But it wasn't the – what is their name? The owners?"

"The Irwins," she informed him.

"Yeah. Well, it wasn't them arguing, that I saw. But the husband came out to stop them."

"Oh." The woman smiled. "Care for a cup of tea? Or...a drink of –"

"No, thank you. I'm sorry to say I forget your name...?"

"Jane."

"Oh, right. I'm bad at names."

"I only just told you five minutes ago!"

"Yes, I am *really* bad with names."

That was the conversation. Randy felt awkward asking her very many questions so he left, pleased, nevertheless.

Would the Irwins be a further problem? He expected so. Most likely the crazy husband had fired the pistol – had been jealous. Hot head.

But the surf beckoned, and he swam right in front of his house, a pleasure most people don't have. Though the water was cold, he took it. He swam around, after passing through the line of waves. A surfer or two caught his attention. With such small waves it struck Randy as improbable they could be enjoying themselves – but you never knew, perhaps they were beginners.

A new day dawned, a pretty one, reminding him of Van Morrison's song "Brand New Day." But the mysterious Irwins invaded his conscious thoughts. What were they actually about? Drug dealers? Communists? Mafia? And who had died?

He kept to himself, going out to the market but saying very little to anyone. He returned with relief, daring to watch the house next door from his upstairs window, after putting the groceries away. No activity in that house, it appeared. Good.

A sense of danger was prevalent, however. Whether it was his imagination or not, who could say? Fear could come from many possible places, real or not real.

Randy found that old box of cigars, left over from he knew not what. A birthday party? But he felt compelled to exact what pleasure he might from smoking one or two.

He saw, first, a Beamer and a Jag pull up to the front of the notorious next-door house. Mr. Irwin, in a pink sport coat, came out of his alley door, directed the parking, and greeted the two couples who emerged from the vehicles.

"Oh, God," Randy thought. "Not another party!" He sat on his couch and smoked one of the cigars, and drank a brandy, dreading the potential for gunshots.

Music poured from the notorious house. Voices were vaguely heard. Non-argumentative, at least. But it was early yet.

Randy switched on his TV and hoped the news programs would distract him from the "party," if it was one.

It distressed him how Carter appeared to be slipping. Would he hang on for another term? The debates were coming soon. Carter had done well against President Ford, in 1976, but Randy knew that Reagan was a swell debater. As a very young man Randy had been impressed by Reagan's debating for governor of California. But no matter how nicely he presented, Reagan's ideas and plans were just too conservative for Randy. And what if he's President, and prods the Soviets into nuclear war? Not likely, certainly, but Randy did not trust him to use diplomacy, as Carter did. Diplomacy was key, in Randy's view, so he leaned toward Carter.

Then stunningly he was awakened, on the couch, by a new gunshot outside his first floor window.

"By God," he said loudly. Forcing himself awake, Randy rose to creep toward the window. But upon arriving and peering out, he could see nothing amiss. He waited, and waited. Finally, deciding it would be dumb, be dangerous, to venture outside to investigate, he made his way upstairs, after checking to see the second cigar was not burning there in the ashtray.

Silence, once again, police cars once again. Randy had undressed, but not completely, and climbed into bed. There just might be a knock on his door, so he waited uneasily.

But there was no knock. Instead he heard words, near the police cars, and the cars driving off. No arrests? No ambulance?

The next morning he jogged over to Jane's house, and called her name. It felt wrong to climb the stairs and search her out boldly. She strode onto the porch, and smiled, seeing him. He yelled:

"Good morning! I have two questions – did you notice the gunfire last night, and what *is* your last name? I don't recall it!"

She laughed. She may be old but she had energy. "My-oh-my, fella. Curious, aren't you?" She continued smiling down at him. "Jogging?"

"Yes," he said, gesturing at his shorts and T-shirt.

"As for your first question, no, I heard no gunfire. Was it from...?" she pointed to the notorious house next to hers.

He nodded. "I believe so."

Jane pursed her lips. "Slept through it, I suppose. As for my last name, it's Marsh."

"Thanks!" Randy ran on; Jane had a perplexed look on her face. But he felt he could explain to her later – possibly after finding out more.

The sun set there to the west, slowly, over the ocean horizon. A few people, a family no doubt, let it go and picked up their beach gear and headed wearily to their car.

Randy watched, a glass of wine in his hand, a pan of hot dogs on the small grill, a glance occasionally to the house next door. How could he approach, gain information?

He wasn't a real detective, after all, private or otherwise. The detectives in books he'd read usually had some sort of authority, and knew what proper questions to ask. He could think of questions, but there was no authority behind them. Wait! There *was*. He heard the shot, he lived right next door, he had a legitimate reason to find out what happened.

So the next morning he went there and climbed the stairs from the beach and knocked on the door, hiding his nervousness.

The husband opened it. He was taller than Randy recalled. There was the start of a mustache on his upper lip.

"Yeah?"

"Hi. I'm, you know, Randy from next door."

"Yeah. Do you want something?"

His attitude was irritating, so Randy grew more forceful.

"Yes, I do. About a couple of nights ago. Noise I heard."

"What noise?"

"Gun going off. What was it?"

Mr. Irwin only hesitated a second, and then smiled. Oh, *that*. Misfire. But it's none of your business."

"Sure it is. I live there." He pointed unnecessarily to his place. "The line of fire, possibly."

"Certainly, so sorry. It won't happen again." He began to close the door. Like all good private detectives, Randy put his foot inside, against it, to block it, but unfortunately he was wearing sandals. Mr. Irwin chuckled. "What?"

"Well," Randy said steadily, "one more question. Weren't the police here again?"

"Yes, but there's no trouble. Now kindly remove your foot or I'll smash it for you!

"Will you?" He kept his foot there.

Irwin made to slam the door. In a split second Randy pulled his foot away, just in time. The door shut forcefully. He breathed a sigh of relief. What next?

Randy moved away, went down the outer staircase to the sand, shaking a little.

He walked up and down in front of a few other houses, pondering the way things were. Something funny going on, but what could he do?

Leave it alone, his practical side instructed. Find out more, his daring side responded. They could be criminals in there, his practical side advised. All the more reason to get to the bottom of it, his stupid side answered.

Wandering back to his house, waving at a jogger near the water, and worrying as he climbed his stairs, for his *safety*, Randy felt nonplussed.

That evening he did a few chores – wrote, read, trimmed his toenails, exercised briefly, showered, sat at peace (sort of) drinking beer. The phone rang once but he let it go to the message machine.

He heard no noise next door. He flipped on the TV, saw local and then national news. Carter's attempt to retrieve the Iran hostages had failed. A surprise raid, but it was called off due to helicopter malfunction. What? *Our* military stymied by that? And then an accident there in the desert rendezvous – loss of life! Mission cancelled. Still, Randy preferred Carter.

And the first Presidential debate didn't appear to help him any. Carter was less confident than four years ago, had less of the gleam in his eye, less of that trademark smile. Reagan won the debate with a confusing plan to help the economy, and cute words like, "There you go again!" Too bad Carter didn't return the line with an emphasis, "There *you* go again," and too bad he didn't counter Reagan's "trickle down" theories more forcefully. Carter wasn't forceful, Reagan was.

It's probably over, Randy thought, except another couple of debates, and Mondale's proficient debating, against Bush this time, *could* keep the Democrats in office, but that crazy Ted Kennedy had undermined the *base*, had turned people against Carter, had refused to campaign for Carter once Kennedy lost in the primaries. Would brother Jack approve of that? No way, Randy concluded.

The days wore on and the hostages remained in Iran, and while the beach was still as beautiful as ever, Randy's spirit was weakening.

By the last days prior to the election, hope of keeping Reagan down looked dim. And as it turned out. Randy voted, for Carter and Mondale, but it was a waste. Well, not a complete waste, because L.A. county leaned against Reagan, even though the state didn't. So his vote counted, sort of.

"Life is full of ups and downs," Randy told himself for several days. In fact, he used that phrase in his nearly completed book, changing it slightly to "Life is rife with ups and downs."

The tide was turning, not only at the beach but all over the world. What could Carter do in his last days in office? Not much.

The war hawks would be in office soon. January loomed on the horizon. Would America survive?

It was cooling off at the beach. Randy's book was being typed up by his usual typist. All was well, more or less. He exercised, paid the housekeeper, watched the news, and movies on VHS, and glanced a little surreptitiously at the house next door. "Peaceful, thank God," he muttered. "Will it stay that way?"

"No telling."

It did, but not very long. In an hour there was a woman (the wife, he presumed) screaming at Mr. Irwin. "Prescott," she shouted, "You - you're lying!"

Randy grimaced. Will the altercation become physical again?

"Calm yourself," Mr. Irwin yelled.

"I say you are lying! Call Nina right now. I want to hear –"

"Shut up! You call her!"

It was quiet. Randy sat on his couch, the patio doors open.

Nothing. Then, further yells, exclamations, and screams. But the two must be in another room, now, because the sounds were muted, the words less clear. Randy put his head in his hands, whispering a long, nearly silent prayer.

Yet there were no gunshots, and then less sounds of voices, at last.

"Peace," he breathed. "Blessed and profound."

The evening passed, the morning came, he drank coffee after a few push-ups and a few sit-ups (twenty apiece).

"Calm yourself," he said. "Things are okay."

But of course they weren't. He found that to be the case when he jogged in the sand by the water, at low tide, that afternoon. There was a shout from that house, and when he looked up he saw a man, presumably Prescott Irwin, tumbling down the outer stairs to the beach. The wife laughed, up above.

Randy stopped his run. He saw that Mr. Irwin was not moving. What to do? Danger was lurking, but being an ex-Army man, and fairly courageous, Randy rushed to the fallen body. And again the wife laughed.

But Irwin was awake, staring up, moaning. "What?" he managed.

"You hurt?" Randy asked.

Not too much, it turned out. A nap and a cocktail revived the fallen man's spirits. The wife busied herself in the kitchen, and had a cocktail herself, just as if nothing had happened. Randy was wondering if he'd be asked to supper, but he wasn't. When asked about what had happened, the wife only shrugged, "He's clumsy. Care for a drink?" He'd been sitting on the sofa for half an hour while Irwin was napping, and she was back in the kitchen. Now, with Irwin downstairs and *their* cocktails in their hands, Randy accepted the offer graciously.

"Whiskey and soda, with ice, please."

"Surely," she replied, smiling.

Next day he pondered the previous day's events. He'd learned nothing very new from the several questions he'd asked them, other than the couple had married in New York City ten years ago, that Mr. Irwin was a retired stockbroker, and fifteen years his wife's senior. She was closed-mouthed regarding the fall down the beach staircase, as was Preston.

"Screw them," Randy spat out as he exercised on his floor, upstairs. "Crazy weirdos."

Sit-ups, push-ups, a drink of water, a look in the refrigerator, a comb through his hair, a promise to shower later, a snatching up of the newspaper on the front mat, a glance up and down the street, and Randy was satisfied the life he had now was swell, so why mix in with weirdo neighbors?

Yep – he'll avoid them.

And now he put bread in the toaster, put the coffee on, went to the bathroom. Swell, swell, swell, he confirmed in his mind. He ate, sat on the deck, napped, and read and had lunch.

Later, he ran, rested, wrote, read more (Rex Stout), wondered about Sophia. He prepared dinner, he watched the news. Not a bad life....

The morning was foggy. Randy didn't mind it, though. Sitting out in it on his deck, wearing warm clothes, was not unpleasant. There was no activity to be noticed next door, and very little on the beach. He still wondered about Sophia, but felt he ought not call her – let it alone.

He wondered who had been wounded that night many months ago. Perhaps Jane had heard more about it. Randy realized he didn't have her phone number. What sort of detective *was* he? But she let him have her number that day, when he visited her in the afternoon. He was nervous for some reason. They spoke inside her house, having tea, as she liked.

Her hair was less gray, now. Perhaps she had darkened it. "Fine foggy day." Randy laughed as they sat at the little table.

"Humm!" she murmured. "Are you well?"

"Oh yes, thank you, Jane. I must say you, too, look well."

"But you say you have another question, besides what is my phone number?" She sipped from her tea cup.

"I do. It's this. Do you suspect drug use next door?"

Jane pursed her lips. "Suspect, yes. But do I know? I'm afraid not."

"Me, either, but there are crazy events happening there. I hope not drug sales or purchases."

"Umm, yes. More tea?" He hadn't finished his cupful.

"No, thank you. But…"

She looked at him expectantly.

"Uh, you know, drug trafficking is particularly dangerous. Violent, I mean. So I've heard. We need to be on our guard."

Jane merely stared at him then nodded after a moment, and sipped at her tea.

So much for that, Randy said to himself.

"I want to sniff around to see them both again, to dig up something, if there is anything. Want to help?"

Jane nodded, and sipped. He sipped. "Like, uh, first I go there, get inside, ask a few questions. About the shooting. They won't care for that, but I'll say you feel frightened. If they wish to call you, I want to encourage it." He watched her. She wasn't nodding, and was pursing her lips. "You'll need to say we've talked and you *are* frightened," he added.

"All right, Mr. Whynn," she agreed. "It sounds good."

Fine, he told himself, so far.

The following day Randy had his plan. Simple. Knock on their door, request a few words with them, or whosoever of them is there, and if he needed to, spring the Jane Marsh "frightened" notion. Wouldn't actually be a lie, to his way of thinking. She *must* be a little frightened, after all.

It worked according to plan. Randy felt like Sam Spade. Preston acted the fool, though, when he brought up the shooting.

"It's not any of your damn business!"

"We've been through this before. I'm next door. The cops have questioned me. Should I call them and say you are being belligerent about the shooting, that you are hiding something?"

Preston paused in his belligerency. Then: "No, no, take it easy. I'll tell you. A former – shall we say – girlfriend, was here, dining with us, and several other friends. She had too much to drink, and berated my wife. 'Old witch," she called her." He stopped, and smiled. Randy wondered once more if Preston had all his marbles. "So...my wife went to the bedroom, returned with a pistol, demanded the woman leave, and...the woman laughed at her. So she fired."

"No arrest?"

"Why, no. We told the cops that Rose had advanced on her in a hostile way and my wife was, uh...prompted to fire. In self-defense."

"Huh?"

"What?"

Randy shook his head. "You must have some pull with the police, for them to accept *that*."

"I do," he plainly stated.

Randy was silent then.

"And don't you forget it," Preston added, and stood. "Get out," he demanded.

Randy stood, perplexed.

"Have I offended you, Mr. Irwin?"

"Not yet, but if you come around asking any more nosy questions..." He walked to the door. "Get out," he repeated.

Randy felt "the better part of valor" indicated a quick retreat, so he went, slightly ashamed but satisfied, mostly, that he knew a few more things.

Morning was foggy again. He didn't care to swim these days, even though a few of them were fairly warm and pleasant, because he knew the sea had become cold – at least too cold for him. Surfers had wetsuits. Of course he *could* have one, but since trying that, years ago, and finding it insufficient, he didn't use one. At that time, he'd tried surfing, and found he was not skilled at it.

So he sat on his porch, he prayed (as he sometimes did) to Jesus Christ for peace and hope and guidance, and felt the power of God in his spirit.

It helped him.

Yet the mysterious goings on next door were never far from Randy's mind. *Someday* he'll find out the truth, discover the closely held secret he surmised was at the bottom of, behind, the gunplay and the arguments, and, yes, the fall Preston Irwin took on his stairs, down to the soft sand. Won't he?

Meanwhile, the agent told him his manuscript was accepted for publishing, as long as editing was done. Most writers didn't care for a publisher to assign an editor to pour over their work, and make changes. But it was a time-honored tradition, included in the contract. Want the money and the publicity push (not to mention the printing of copies for stores)? Go along with the editor's alterations, and accept the final outcome. Randy knew from experience that resisting any changes was usually counter-productive. Best not aggravate your publisher!

So he reveled in the news, coping with the pang of dreading the editing. He could live with that; he had little choice.

Then a day went by, Jasmine cleaned the house, did laundry, even prepared a meal for Randy, and left with a smile and a wave as he paid her and thanked her. She was young, brown-haired, slightly plump – and happy-spirited.

Now, what to do, he wondered, drinking beer and watching the news. After a half-hour of that, he checked the old movie channel, not finding things he cared to see.

Randy did have a collection of the old Naked City episodes, but that didn't appeal to him. He watched the news.

Stuff about Reagan, of course, boring to him. The hostages were free, of course – that was good.

He turned off the T.V., pulled a Zane Grey western off his shelf – "Majesty's Rancho" – and read. Or rather, re-read.

But then around midnight more gunfire from next door. He dropped to the floor, an old army tactic – if fighting erupted. He heard three shots and he waited, on the floor.

But nothing. No yells, no screams, no breaking glass. What had happened, he wondered? Did he need to call the police? Maybe, but he held off. Those people next door were weird, and *anything* may have transpired – including foolish indoor "target practice."

So, as silence ensued, he went to bed, to sleep fitfully. In the morning, he would go over there – or at least ask Jane about it. Perhaps. Because the entire play of events regarding the Irwins troubled and repelled him, ought he leave it all alone? He wanted to! Why be involved any more? What did he care if they murdered each other?

Well, he *cared*, but not enough to risk getting murdered himself.

Dawn arrived. He exercised. He showered. He ate. He took coffee to his patio. He glanced next door but saw no one. The waves broke, small waves. A few joggers went by at the water's line. It was peaceful.

Randy fought the desire to go ask Jane if she'd heard the shots, and what she thought (if she had). Maybe Jane had information he didn't. Unquestionably, manifestly, he was somehow drawing away from the mysterious and dangerous gloom that hovered over the next house. A conflict between his curiosity and his safety now tended to pull in the direction of safety. Personal safety has its place, does it not?

"Yes," he told himself. "My curiosity can be controlled!"

And so it was for many days, and nights.

He smoked cigars, he drank beer, he went to the market, he awaited news of the editing of his novel, he watched the T.V., he watched the horizon, he watched the house next door out of the corner of his eye. Peace reigned, generally. But for how long?

Also he watched a cute girl on the beach, on a towel. She never seemed to notice him. Brown hair, slender, maybe 21 years old, or so. Randy decided to jog, which he did, and waved to her when he passed by, up at the water line. She waved back. He might have been more aggressive and approached her, to talk, but no, that didn't seem right. If he ever saw her again on the beach, *then* he'd approach and strike up a conversation. He didn't want to frighten her, or make her more wary of him than she may be anyway, considering he was a stranger. Although he knew based on past experience that women were more agreeable to being approached when on a beach, in such a pleasant setting, than in other places. Maybe because they were only partially dressed? It seemed surprising, but who could figure women out? Not Randy.

The police didn't come by to ask him about the shooting, this time. He'd definitely go to speak with Jane soon. Meanwhile he watched the news and a movie, "The Omega Man," on VHS. Having studied the Bible some, in years past, Randy knew the word Omega denoted "last" in the Greek. How many people knew that, how many people knew it meant the Charlton Heston part, the character, was the "last" man, supposedly? Anyway he enjoyed the science-fiction movie. It took his mind off the neighbors, temporarily.

But that mysterious house was there, still, the next morning. Randy never had liked it, with its overhanging roof, dark wood, etc. Like a house on the "edge," he thought, with a certain sense of concealment, although on the brink of such openness (on the ocean). It was no closer to the ocean, or further away, than his own house, but the place felt divorced from the other ones near it. And so it was, in fact, in some way.

Randy saw the fine-looking woman again, putting on sunblock, ignoring other beach-goers. It was warm for that time of year, and folks were taking advantage of the weather before the nippy spring coastal temperatures replaced this warm spell. Randy knew he ought to take advantage of the moment, and he did. He strolled to the water, stepping in, in his beach shorts, and turned. Walking past the woman he smiled and said, "No way! It's too cold for a swim!"

She nodded perfunctorily, and he made one more attempt at sociability. "Do you live nearby? My place is there," pointing to it.

"Oh, my friends do. Staying with them." She gestured slightly with her head, at nothing much in particular.

"My name is Randy Whynn. But," he continued when she failed to supply her own, "not that house there, I hope." He pointed to the mysterious neighbors' place.

She looked over, she shook her head, she watched Randy with cautious green eyes. "I would say not! Don't like that place."

"Really!" He boldly sat beside her. "Can I ask why?"

She watched him. She made a decision. He seemed like a nice fellow, well-built and calm. "Frankly those...they scare me."

"Wow. They scare me, too."

She laughed. "You've had trouble with them?

"A bit. Recently there was a shooting, but I don't know any details." She nodded.

He waited, then asked, "Have you met the residents?"

She sighed. "Out in front, there, the woman told me to move away from their house. She said to move away!" The green eyes flashed. "Can you beat that?"

"Well, I don't care for either of them, if it's any comfort to you."

She only stared, then looked away. "Another thing, you seem to be a gentleman. The husband isn't. I guess he's the husband. He whistled at me, another day. Rudely, I thought."

"Umm. Sorry."

"Don't think I can't take care of myself, Randy. I can. But they – well, they scare me somehow."

"Sure."

They left it at that, aside from her telling him to call her Bev. Bev Martinson. He didn't want to be involved if she should ask him to protect her. A crazy thought, certainly, yet Randy felt she *would* ask him to protect her. She was just that weird, he sensed.

He ate lunch morosely. The housekeeper fiddled around, cleaning, and washing dishes, and left at four. Napping was difficult. He'd given Bev his phone number, she'd put it in a small notebook in her beach bag. He rolled off his bed, not having slept, but perhaps ten minutes. If she called, what kind of conversation would they have?

Maybe: "This is Bev Martinson."

"Oh, yes, hello."

"I need help. I just got stabbed by that nasty woman for sunbathing too close to her house, and her husband –"

"Stop! Tell me no more."

No, no, that's not how the conversation will go…

Randy chugged a beer.

If she called, he'd be cool.

And cool he was. Bev telephoned two days later, while the sun was setting, and he was idling on his patio sipping water, staring at the horizon. He went inside to answer his phone, said "Hello?" and tensed up when she gave her name. But he forced himself to cool down.

"What's up?" he asked, as casually as he could.

"Something important. Or not, as may be."

"Cryptic, Bev."

"Okay, listen to this. My friend – you know, who is putting me up here, knows the Irwins."

"Uh-huh...."

"She told me about them. They are spies of some kind for the government."

"Far out. I always have wanted to meet a spy."

Bev paused. That crack didn't go over well with her.

"Hello?" he said.

"Listen. They are capable of anything. A government spy can break in, can steal, can kill if they want to, and fade away."

"So...."

"So take care, Randy. I like you. Keep away from them."

"Right." He laughed.

"What's so funny?"

"Here I was thinking you would want me to challenge them, to tell them to not bother you, and I...well...."

"You wanted to protect me?"

"Kind of, but...oh heck. I wanted to weasel out of it. Sorry."

"You beast!"

"Blame me?"

"No, I'm kidding."

"Good."

"Call me – don't wait too long. Will you update me if...there's something?"

"Most certainly."

Time slowly passed, as it can when nothing very exciting or interesting occurs. How Randy longed to charge up those creepy stairs and pound on the door and demand to know, are y'all intelligence agents? What's your bloody job, anyway?

But naturally, he couldn't do that. Too dangerous. Intelligence agents function in secret, have lots of money at their disposal, and are trained to deal effectively with obstructions to their operations. And breaking laws means nothing to them. At least, Randy had picked up this information from watching Congressional hearings, from newspapers, and from James Bond films.

What Randy needed to do, wanted to do, was find out why Bev's friends thought the Irwins were agents: how reliable was their information?

He watched the creepy house from his upstairs window, late in the evening. He made sure his doors were all locked, and his windows as much as possible. Of course locks and latches were child's play for intelligence operatives – even FBI agents, probably. But he slept soundly. Randy was generally a brave person.

Dawn brought hope. After exercise and breakfast, Randy spoke on the phone to Bev. She agreed to ask her friends the source of their curious information about the next door neighbors. That would provide Randy with some satisfaction.

It was a chilly day; he decided not to jog, or even to walk, on the beach. The temptation to look at the house might be too much for him, and God knows what cameras the spies had up there.

Surveillance is as common with intelligence activities as collars on pets, Randy surmised. And those two odd people may consider him a person to watch out for.

In two hours Bev called, informing him the couple she was staying with refused to disclose the source of their "spies" pronouncement. The man asked why Bev wanted to know, and she'd felt compelled to lay it on Randy. The woman thought it was funny, telling her husband that curiosity was natural. The man, Rex, still didn't like it. "Stop spreading this around," he'd told Bev.

"Umm," Randy replied. "Care is called for here. Please leave it alone and let me think this over."

"Okay. Will do."

Tough, thinking it over. What the hell to do? Care was sure called for, but some sort of approach must obviously be conducted. He pondered it.

An idea finally came. He'd head for the house, go up, knock on the door, and ask them, whoever answered, for a "word, please." He'd go inside, tell them, both or one of them, that he, being a writer, wanted help. Have they ever worked for the government? If so, how so? He'd say he needed information, whatever they'd provide him, to plan the plot of a story he was writing. That's the way to discern if they were actually spies or not – he could tell from their own mouths!

Well, maybe.

Anyway, the good thing was he'd be telling the truth – he decided then and there to write a story with government agents in it. That awareness could aid Randy when asking the Irwins for assistance.

Yet, while walking next door, he began to get cold feet. Was he risking his life? Could be.

So he hesitated, paused, had to get a grip on himself. It wouldn't do to be nervous, or shaky. *Confident*, that was the correct method. If not, they'd likely know something was up, and if suspicious, who knows what the Irwins were capable of?

Randy didn't have long to wait, for as he started up the outer staircase, Mrs. Irwin showed herself at the top. She was wearing a bathing suit, one piece, and had no doubt been sunning herself when seeing his approach. Or had she? How could she have seen him if lying down on the porch? There was a long row of potted plants at the edge. But that question wasn't concerning Randy now. More immediately, he must smile and say hello, and ask her permission to climb up. Which feat he accomplished. She made way for him, curiosity showing on her face.

The afternoon went well, in spite of Randy's nervousness. Mrs. Irwin made it no easier by her suspicious eyes, her firm mouth, her care in answering questions.

Mr. Irwin never showed up. Randy pressed the wife, and in fact received several interesting replies. She acknowledged having been a low-level congressional aide, and her husband too, many years back. Beyond such revelations she wouldn't go, yet Randy surmised her eyes held darker secrets. So be it.

His claim to be writing a story involving secret government activity produced a few results. She said there was a hidden power structure in Washington, answerable to the president. What was it, he asked? "Operations I can't reveal to you. Not that I was a part! No way."

"Criminal?"

"Depends on your point of view," she guardedly replied.

"Can't you tell me more?"

"No," Mrs. Irwin announced. "Perhaps I've told you too much already." She sipped her drink. "Anyway, I need to change. Preston will be here shortly. I must prepare supper."

He took the cue, rising, and downing the rest of his bourbon and soda. "Okay, no sweat. Thanks for helping me. I can use what you've told me in my story." He smiled. That was the end of it. He left, relieved.

Not that he'd found out much. They may be spies, or they may not.

After a report to Bev, time flowed along peacefully. What else could he do? One day, two days, three days. Jasmine came and cleaned, the beach sported very few bathers (too cold), the waves continued to crash.

He waited anxiously for the novel editor's report. He ate he drank he read he exercised he watched T.V. he glanced furtively at *that* house, he slept.

He also went out to the market. He liked doing it. Why? It provided him with time away from his constant surroundings – the porch, the rest of the house, the beach, the water, and now, the neighbors. The weird neighbors.

The day came when Sophia called. She was okay, apparently. No difficulty, no tragedy, no bruises. He withstood the impulse to invite her over – that could bring trouble. Randy wanted no more trouble of any kind. It was, nevertheless, fine and dandy to speak with her – he liked Sophie.

Later he heard the Irwins arguing, but not for long. Gratefully there were no gunshots, yet he did worry. He drank beer, he watched the news and a sitcom, bearing the strain.

Life can be both good and bad, he figured. God has his ways. We can't fathom all of these tribulations, these difficulties, that "beset" us. Randy faced his future with hope, anyway. Jesus loves us, he knew. He died for us – that's love. If the neighbors caused Randy trouble, he'd have to pray and ask God for help, no two ways about it. He slept well that night.

But he felt nervous in the morning. Things looked bleaker in the light of day. He wanted to call Bev. He wanted to have sex with her. He even wanted her to spend the night, be fond of him, fry him eggs, smile at him over coffee. But was he willing to have it go wherever it would go, if he made the attempt? Randy thought about her, and decided, yes. Most definitely.

With a caveat – she'd bail out when she saw how uninterested he was in marriage. Or, she wouldn't. After all Randy was a sort of free spirit, no? Nearly a beachcomber, if you discounted the expensive house! So she might accept him as that, as he was at heart and soul. If she didn't, if she negated the relationship when finding out he was unwilling to marry, so be it.

Dawn suddenly arrived. What had happened to the day prior? Gone fast. Randy grimaced as he pulled out of bed. Time for water on the face. And a series of push-ups, and sit-ups, as normally. But soon he pictured Bev, her lithe body, her penetrating eyes, her sweet-looking mouth. Oh how was he ever going to deal with her? He was not a ladies man, he was a slow-thinking beach bum. Or nearly.

It was cold. It suited him, though. Hot beach weather can get old. A brisk breeze in the face made Randy happy to be alive. He jogged awhile, avoiding looking at that crazy house.

Inside *his* house, he showered and flipped on the TV. But shortly Randy was upstairs, gazing surreptitiously through narrowly divided curtains. No action next door, he noted. In a few minutes, he returned to his TV, the local news. His day wound down, like an ancient watch.

Randy wanted to call Bev. But she saved him the actual effort by placing a call herself. In the morning.

"Hello, you," she intoned. "What are you up to?"

"Not much. Thinking about the outline of a new novel. And you?"

"Hoping to make a hasty exit, if you can believe it. My friends are arguing a lot. I don't care for it. Nasty words are floating around. I want to escape."

Randy bit his tongue as a wish to invite her to move in crossed his mind suddenly. No, no, he told himself.

"Gee, that's tough," he replied instead. "When?" It was all he could think of to ask.

"As soon as...tomorrow. But we should speak, first, concerning you-know-what."

"The weirdos?"

"Yes. I have more information. You need to hear this."

"Ah! Well, then, come over anytime you want. I'm just hanging out."

"Fine. First some packing, and a chat with my friends."

"Fine," he replied.

"See you later, Randy."

"Okay." She cut the phone connection, slamming the receiver down forcefully. She was excited, he thought to himself. *Too* excited. What had happened over there?"

Bev showed up, hair askew, no lipstick, an old blouse, blue jeans, no shoes.

"A drink, please!" she begged upon entering. Randy wanted to hug her, but dared not.

"What?" he asked. "Booze or beer?"

She smiled. "I thought beer *was* booze."

"In my circle, no. But let's not quibble. Scotch, brandy, whiskey?"

"Beer."

Well, well, well, he thought to himself. Marrying her mightn't be a good idea – she's a wise ass.

But anyway, he brought her beer, poured it in a glass. She sipped at it with gusto. He joined her, pouring another one, sipping it peacefully. She had something to say – it was up to her when. It was no doubt very important.

Finally the words came: "Oh my God. You won't believe it, Randy."

He sipped, but his heart raced now. What wouldn't he believe? She stared past his head and said, "I am a very bad girl. I stole a ring from Cathy. She discovered it hidden in my belongings. The snoop!"

"Hidden?" He wanted to say, "Stole?" but skipped that part, for now. Bev was still glancing away.

"*Well* hidden," she murmured, practically to herself.

"I see." When she said nothing further, he asked, "Expensive?"

She only nodded her head, but then turned her fearful eyes on him, when he said, "This is crazy!"

"Umm, right," she intoned listlessly, her brown eyes now somber, not fearful. "Will you, I mean, speak with them? Tell them to forget it, that I am sorry, that you know me, that...stuff to calm them down?"

"I could. In fact, why not?

"It won't be easy. They might find it hard to believe it means nothing, that you didn't intend to keep the ring."

"That's a fine idea! I only wanted to wear it, alone, for fun."

"Yes, it *could* sound all right. Did you really believe you'd get away with it, Bev?"

"Frankly, honestly, no. I felt scared, but..." her eyes closed as she sought for the expression: "...compelled."

"Umm, yes."

"But damn it, they could press charges!"

"I thought you were long time friends," Randy reminded her.

She nodded, and tears came.

He provided a tissue box for her, quickly.

"Thanks." She then dabbed her eyes.

"It will work out," he told her, and turned to watch the setting sun paint the sky rose.

It *did* work out. He was taken to the large beach house of her friends, the Burtons. They cordially accepted the introduction, and Bev disappeared upstairs. The three sat in a plush, un-beach-like living room. Ginger ale was provided when Randy declined the offer of harder stuff. The Burtons drank iced tea.

"What's the deal?" Mr. Burton bluntly asked, his tall frame shifting.

"The ring," Randy announced.

The couple were silent.

"She's sorry. She couldn't help herself. Possibly a form of kleptomania."

"Such as you say, Mr. Whynn," the wife Cathy, a small woman with blonde hair and pinched brows, evidencing a frown, said. "Still, what is it to you?"

"Oh, we have known each other...awhile, and I wish to vouch for her. Not saying she should continue living here – that's up to you folks. But as for criminal charges, I dispute the need." He was speaking like a lawyer in one of his books. "She is asking for your forgiveness and good graces to...to not press, um, charges." He shut up, then, believing he'd said enough.

And so it went, the Burtons drank their tea and looked at each other, and finally agreed. It would be "forgotten," Rex Burton avowed.

Of course, Bev would move out, but she didn't want to return to her house, the one she'd been in before, due to "turmoil," as she called it. Her mother and stepfather got along, that wasn't the issue. It was her, she was just too "wild," they thought. And being in close contact with them grated on her. It was the main reason she'd moved in with the Burtons, long time family friends – to escape her home.

She'd paid for food but the Burtons extracted no rent from her. Her plans to train in real estate were forestalled. It *was* the beach, after all. And perhaps she wasn't *that* interested in real estate sales…

But would that man put her up? Would he request sex? Would Bev be okay with that? She couldn't decide. It would all depend on how she felt about him when and if the time came.

"Are you going to stay with me?" he asked out of the blue, when she made her way down the beach stairs, a suitcase in hand, with Randy behind, struggling with two cases himself. He nearly fell on the stairs, but recovered his balance, asking the question before reaching the bottom.

She turned to face him, her eyes firm. "Yes, if I might."

"You might," he said, smiling.

Where she'd stay, his room, or another, remained an open question until ten that night. It was quickly decided as he led her by the hand to his bedroom, asking, "Should I put one of your suitcases in here?"

"Better do so. The red one."

He did it and stood silent, waiting for any indication of yea or nay, stay or go, from her. His own feelings were leaning to "yea," and "stay," but yet, a vote is provided to a woman, in his view.

On the edge of uncertainty, also leaning to a yea, especially due to the wine Randy had provided her, Bev wished he'd made the decision for them. She liked a confident man, not a weak one. But his nature was not to push, to force, women. She watched him, she held her breath, she let a light smile play over her lips.

That look was enough for him. He approached, he took her by her shoulders, he pressed his lips to hers. She allowed him to, gladly.

So it was.

In the morning they went out on the patio after having breakfast, which they'd prepared together. Bev was somber – this was a new part of her life, a new "journey," so to speak. Randy felt happy, something he'd missed since Sophia, yet not realizing that until this day.

They watched the little waves, the gray horizon, the seagulls.

A week of their happiness led them into a bit of rain, and noise from the neighbors' house. Mr. Irwin shouting, that was apparent. And his wife shouting back. The words were indistinct but for one full-throated bellow, "Horse's ass!!" from Mr. Irwin, and a screamed, "Keep your damn hands off me!" from Mrs. Irwin.

Bev and Randy exchanged looks. Fear, distress, even a tiny bit of humor.

"What now?" they wondered.

Randy shook his head. "They fight so much."

Bev said nothing.

"Too much," he continued, as if that held a significant meaning. And it did. The two, in one house, cringed at the idea of a gunshot happening in the other. But it didn't. At least, not that day. The next day, yes.

Morning was pleasant. Bev seemed adjusted to the surroundings, the new closeness of a partly unknown presence in her life, and Randy felt similarly. Waking up with a smiling woman never did a man any harm, as far as he knew. He silently thanked God, but didn't have the courage to tell Bev about his gratitude, as likewise she withheld *her* feelings that way.

It was too cold to eat on the patio, so they breakfasted inside. It was just as well considering what happened that morning. Mr. Irwin fell, again, down the stairs to the beach, as someone fired a shot.

Randy rushed to his door, seeing the man's final plunge onto the sand. A second shot rang out, and Mr. Irwin moaned, becoming still. The laugh Randy knew so well rang out – Mrs. Irwin defiantly crouching at the top of the stairs, pistol in hand, a diabolical grin creasing her face bizarrely.

"Bev! Call the police!" Randy ran to retrieve one of his own pistols, and then returned to his spot inside the door, seeing Mrs. Irwin retreat into the house. Mr. Irwin didn't move, even slightly.

The aftermath was predictable. Police listened to Randy and Bev's description of events, approached the house warily, apprehended Mrs. Irwin when she claimed responsibility, after, the police confirming the body on the sand was deceased.

Interviews at the station, papers to sign, various officers to speak with. At home, quite late, they swallowed sandwiches and beer, barely speaking, falling into bed, embracing, thankful the hard day required nothing else.

They had not mentioned the suspicion the Irwins were government agents. The police would find it out, or not, but it wasn't Randy or Bev's business anyway. Why she shot him, the police had to figure out – not Randy and Bev. Actually, Randy didn't care, and Bev, who was curiouser, didn't care very much. They felt relief that the next door ordeal, for them, was apparently resolved. Or so they thought.

Time passed. They liked each other, they disputed, about anything, very little.

She was happy. Randy joked, tried to lighten the mood. A professional housecleaning team showed up next door, made noise cleaning the house, taking hours to accomplish it. Mrs. Irwin was nowhere to be seen, but that made sense if she'd been charged and yet granted no bail.

"That place needs a good cleansing," he told Bev when the crew drove away in their truck.

"You got that right," Bev quipped.

A few days later, however, two men in beach attire forced the lock on the street side, and entered the house. Bev saw them do it from the bedroom window, and ran to inform Randy in the kitchen. He went to the window, looking, and yet saw, heard, nothing. Then, a moment later, the men appeared on the patio and stared at the sea.

"Approach them?" he asked Bev.

"Oh, my God, no," she replied.

"But I want to find out what is going on."

"Sure, but if they are spies, too, you –" She stopped talking.

"But I want to know!"

She had no response to that.

"I want to find out something one way or another."

"All right. Don't let me stop you," she replied.

He went out the door and yelled to the men, "Hello, guys. What's happening?"

They both turned to face him, scowling. Not happy people. When there was no response, Randy asked, "Are you raiding the place?"

Once again they didn't speak. One, the taller one, smiled. His hair was thinning, showing gray, and his eyes were pinched. The other, younger, well-built, red-haired, opened his mouth, but then closed it.

"Should I call the police? Do you have the right to be there?" Still they didn't answer. Randy thought, they're dressed, shorts and T-shirts, like they are pretending to belong. But they have no tans, he observed. He walked to the side of his patio, as near to these quiet men as he could be, on his property. They *might* have guns in their back pockets, he realized, so further demands and threats were ill-advised on his part.

"Uh..." he began. "Have you heard from...Mrs. Irwin?" Frustratingly, they wouldn't answer. "Just wondering. Last I saw, the cops took her away after, uh, an unpleasant incident."

The shorter one, with red hair, laughed out loud. His partner gave him a severe look.

"Okay, you guys. I tried." Randy turned, walking to his door, and safely went inside. Bev stood motionless – "frozen," as it were.

"Call the cops?" he asked.

"You bet I did."

The result was weak; the men left prior to the police arrival. Randy had run to the alley front window to try to get their car's license plate number, but was too late, as they sped off quickly. He described the car, and the men to the police, however. Bev asked a couple of questions but was met with unsatisfactory replies. No, they couldn't say if Mrs. Irwin had a connection to the intruders – how could they know? They took the report and departed, warning against any further confrontation should those men reappear.

As if they would! They'd be too smart to do that. They might be spies, mightn't they? What they'd been doing in the house – looking for something? – was another mystery. But that question prompted Bev and Randy to worry: perhaps the men *would* return.

"Just keep away from them, if they do," she urged. "They may go crazy if we prevent them their, their...purpose."

"Right, honey. You are quite correct."

And they *did* return, at night, with flashlights. Randy tried to get the license plate number, again, but since the front of the place, on the "street," was not well-lit, he couldn't.

They locked their doors, they waited, armed with Randy's pistol, and hoped for the best. They saw moving lights inside the house as the two men obviously searched it, and finally left, driving off in a hurry.

Bev and Randy breathed sighs of relief, hugging, smiling, and even finding grace to laugh, as minutes passed by, gradually.

The following day it was calm on the beach, on the porch, even next door.

Normal again. *Until*, of course, the potential trial, and subpoenas to testify. Both Bev and Randy? Only one of them? Time would tell. And also, suddenly one day, professional-looking movers came to take furniture and boxes out of that house.

It was beginning to warm up, yet there was rain, some days. Bev was glad Jasmine came by, because she didn't like housekeeping. Randy still considered her a house guest, so that was no problem. They still slept in his bed, with accompanying behavior. Bev was, nevertheless, somewhat shy about it, because she feared he would fall in love with her – which she didn't want. She didn't want any major attachments. She liked freedom. Randy could "have" her, that was fine, but he couldn't possess her.

Time flew. He got deep into the edits of his book by the publisher. That didn't make him happy, but he knew he was in no position to argue much. Publishers held the power.

"I bet something happened, that there will be no murder trial," he told Bev.

"Huh? What?"

"Maybe she escaped, or the spy network had her released. Who knows what intelligence agencies are capable of?"

Bev had to agree with him. "Then I suppose we won't testify...."

"Well, I can call that cop who took statements from us...." He stared out at the water. They were sitting on the porch. "He *may* tell me what's going on."

And he did, informing Randy that the woman was freed "on a technicality. That's how it goes once in awhile."

"But, heck, what's behind it?"

"Listen. There are some things better left alone." The cop hung up.

Bev didn't like it. "What the hell?"

"Better left alone," Randy repeated, bitterly. "That's his viewpoint. His official opinion. Things are better left alone."

"It doesn't take a genius to know spies are behind it," Bev said, sipping her cold drink. "One way or another."

Deadlines

Not working for a news organization, he didn't in fact have to push the pace to finish his letter to his boss, but Archie couldn't help it – he felt pressured. Quitting a job was not easy. But he worked fast, he listed reasons, made apologies, signed it, folded it, placed it in an envelope. A grin crossed his mouth and quickly vanished.

Rising, Archie hitched aside the briefcase. He wouldn't be needing that anymore. He made it to the front room, pushed open an office door, and entered. Caruso, of course, was not inside at this hour. The desk was there, though, and he dropped the envelope on it. He glanced around. Everything appeared in order, but what did that matter now?

He took his car, feeling rushed, still, and picked up sandwiches at a deli nearby, entered his apartment building, hoofed it up the two flights of stairs rather than taking the elevator, for no good reason, and let himself in. The deed was done.

Freedom may come in various forms. With a cushion of money in the bank, Archie found freedom as gratifying as expected, but for one thing: nobody to share it with. Part of the cause of his quitting had been the failed relationship with the boss's daughter. He'd wanted out of her way, he wanted to escape any memory. Not easily done, since it was not at work that he'd seen her – at least not often. But she'd occasionally stopped by to see her father, and the receptionist she was friendly with, and to glance knowingly in Archie's direction if he happened to emerge from his own office. That was all well and good, *before*. But not now that their romance had faded.

In the morning he rolled out of bed, at once thinking he had to go to work, but then recalled he didn't. Archie had not given notice, he had abruptly quit. The boss wouldn't care, he would easily replace a lower-level operative, a minor gumshoe in a large detective business. There were two detectives over him, and another operative who had done most of the fieldwork. Archie was basically a back-up, calling and emailing clients and individuals associated with the cases the Horn Detective Service was working on. Yes, he had a P.I.'s license, but hadn't used it often. Now, would he ever?

Archie was thirty years old, five foot ten, one hundred sixty pounds. Now unemployed. But he felt good. He could find other work.

A little problem presented itself. The barbershop he frequented was closed, a fact Archie learned the next day when he went there for a haircut. "Closed until further notice," the sign on the front door rather rudely declared.

Instead, he proceeded to the market, bought eggs and beer, and returned to his apartment.

Archie was hungry. The toast and coffee he'd had first thing wasn't enough to last until lunch. But the container of leftover rice and beans, combined with two eggs he now fried was.

Holding on to tradition, he received a daily newspaper delivery, so while he ate, he read. To Archie's surprise, a murder had been committed the day before at his favorite barbershop. One of the barbers, found dead in the evening by the regular cleaning crew. Then it was difficult for him to swallow, so he ceased eating as he read the news article. Well...that explained the shop's closure. An investigative team from the police department, complete with coroner, had no doubt spent part of the night examining the scene and the body, and taken photos, removing the body, and probably calling in the shop's owner and possibly, staff.

Archie could contact a friend in the police department to ascertain, possibly, more facts, but he hesitated. Should he, now, out of the agency? A private individual with no real official standing? And he also hesitated because he wasn't so sure he cared to find out more. Yes, he was curious, but simply being a customer was hardly cause for a determined effort, was it?

His detective sensibility won over. He called his friend on the homicide squad, Ralph Carpenter, a black sergeant.

"I know about the situation, yes," Ralph told him."Not that the lieutenant would care for me sharing it with you!"

"Just the basic details, not the details of your full investigation."

"Well, what do you care? Were you there that day?"

"Oh, no, but I knew that barber."

"Uh-huh," Ralph murmured.

"And?"

"His name was Trout, as you may know. He was shot in the head at close range. He died immediately. A wife and two kids."

"Thanks. The paper said that. But who did it? Any suspects?"

"Oh, as to that...the door was unlocked, so anyone *may* have come in on him. But to get so close, probably someone he knew."

"Or, the shooter drew and pointed the gun at him, and approached," Archie suggested.

"Sure."

"And there are no witnesses? Anyone nearby hear the shot?"

"Not as far as we've found."

"Did he have enemies? Did the boss like him?"

"No enemies, well liked at work," Ralph replied.

"Yes, that was my impression. But *somebody* didn't care for him."

"No. And no one reported seeing anyone entering or leaving the building after it was closed." Ralph added, his face cracking a smile.

"Oh! I forgot to ask that. Must be rusty, not being a detective now."

Ralph laughed. "But just after two days? Anyway, that's all we know. Not much."

In the car going toward the apartment, the whole deal felt hopeless. If the cops were getting nowhere with their resources, *he* sure couldn't...and he knew his own methods were less effective since he'd sworn off lying. Telling mistruths was a distasteful part of detective work, and one of the reasons he'd quit. Archie didn't like telling lies. Pretending he was someone he wasn't, tricking people. Investigating crimes, particularly murder, was hard, anyway, without having to be honest about it! But Archie was dead serious about being honest. If it got him no place, then so be it.

But where to start? At the barbershop. Questioning the staff. Most of them he knew, so....

It didn't turn out too well. The staff had clammed up, weary of the police asking questions. One of the barbers, or the manicurists, or the boss even, could be the murderer, and none of them (except possibly one) was feeling "safe." Who might be next? Archie got little from his visit and questioning. Except Markie, the oldest barber, told him how the cops had been asking about a Glock, did any of them own one? So Archie was confident that was the murder gun, a fact Ralph had refused to reveal.

A detective has to deduct, you know.

Also he questioned the one manicurist on duty, Faye, a small thirtyish woman with bright blonde hair. She was clammed up too, although he used his charm, his smile, and she weakened enough to say, "There have been problems here, of late. Ask the boss. He knows about it." Archie had decided to let that go, for the time being. It was a very interesting lead, but he didn't care to press his luck *or* his welcome, now. He'd return for a haircut, and ask the boss about any "problems." Might lead somewhere.

Meanwhile, he carried on with a life of non-attachment to any employer – except perhaps himself. Who had killed the barber was a question which intrigued him, but it wasn't precisely an assignment.

After a few days, Archie went to the shop, got a haircut from Markie. He didn't see Faye, and he didn't see Henry, the boss. But he decided to ask Markie about the "trouble" he'd heard about, saying it was the "word he'd picked up," in private detective parlance. Markie was guarded:

"What kind of trouble?"

"Uh, conflict, arguments, things like that...."

So Archie retrieved his jacket from the rack behind the chair, and his barber said, "I wouldn't tell you even if I knew what –"

"I understand," Archie interrupted. "But, in strict confidence?"

Markie paused a moment. "I like you, sir. You always tip, you always smile, you are a good regular patron. *But* let's say Henry would blow a gasket if he found out I told you."

Archie glanced around. No eavesdroppers were within range. "Give me a hint, won't you?"

"Sure, I will. A girl and a guy get together, but when her husband learns of it, he storms in here and punches well, someone."

"Who?"

"Not me, but...another barber." He walked away, saying, "That's it."

"Yeah, that's it." Archie said to himself: "The husband did it."

But he couldn't go to Ralph without any corroboration. The boss was Archie's next target.

He needed to handle it right, of course, so for the next day he pondered the possibilities, approaching Henry without exposing Markie as the source. He came up with a plan and returned to the barbershop.

Several customers were being attended to in the three barbers' chairs, and one in the manicurist's cubicle, Faye doing the honors. She smiled at him as he passed over to the front counter with Henry behind it, looking official, proud to be the boss (if not the main owner, his Uncle Leo, long retired).

"Hello," Archie said. "How are you?"

Henry nodded. "Fair, Mr. Gordon. May I help you?"

"Well, the police are questioning the reason for my interest in the...Fred Trout shooting, and I need to ask you something."

Henry said nothing.

"It's a problem, the fact that I know who killed Trout, but don't want to tell them."

All that was true, basically, as Archie saw it. Henry's eyebrows went up.

"I know the manicurist's husband did the shooting. Are you aware of that?"

"Say, Mr. Gordon, what – how could I know that?"

"It makes sense. Of course, you were aware of the romance here, and the jealous husband, and –"

"Stop! Who told you that?"

"Never reveal my sources, Henry. Surely you know I'm a detective?"

"Sure, yeah. But do the police know about the, uh, affair? Between...?"

"They do not. Yet."

The boss looked grim, his lips compressed. Archie smiled at him. "No need to worry, I won't tell, unless it does turn out that the affair led to the killing, as I suspect, and in fact, believe. But police don't need my conjectures. The question is, why so afraid of them knowing Trout was screwing – what's her name, anyway?"

Henry turned away – a customer was approaching to pay. After that transaction, Archie stood expectantly, waiting for answers to his queries. But none came. Henry waved him off, grunting, "Get out of here. I have nothing more to say."

So who was the woman? Hopefully, Archie could ask Faye, and receive a good answer. If so, he was one step closer to a solution that would hold up to Ralph's scrutiny.

He went to the manicurist's cubicle. Both women were busy, with two middle-aged gentlemen. No hope there. His plans required privacy. An appointment? But he might, still, be overheard by another customer. It was a chance that must be taken. A good detective needs to take chances. He made the appointment for the next day, with the other one – not Faye. Henry frowned at him, but entered it in the computer anyway. Archie just *had* to find out what the manicurist knew: Elena. He'd barely spoken with her, had mostly nodded her way a few times.

The direct approach? Ask her about the shooting? Call her bluff if she denied any knowledge beyond what others knew? He could say he's working independently, with no client, only curious. Would she open up? Probably no but it was worth trying. Smile, he told himself.

So, up the staircase and into his apartment, pop a bottle of beer, remove his shoes, grimace at the day to come. He would need beer.

Sipping the beer, Archie knew he was on shaky ground. If Elena's husband had killed Trout, *and she knew it*, she could tell that murderer he was in danger of discovery, and the "discoverer" may not live long. The risk of that was only moderate, and could be partly manageable based on the signs shown by Elena, as *their* conversation proceeded.

Archie slept fairly well, and in the morning ate a hearty breakfast after jogging on the street.

He began to get nervous as he drove to the shop for the appointment. He'd be courting danger, but how much was anyone's guess.

Inside he nodded hello to Markie on the way to see Elena. She had chairs, a table, paraphernalia, a nice smile. Archie was on time. He sat. She asked how he was, he replied pleasantly. She took one hand, viewed his nails, and began the treatment. Archie passed the time with her on pointless subjects – weather, etc. – then struck her with the real topic:

"Someone was killed here? A barber? I knew him, but not very well."

"Um-hmm," she offered. "Sad." Her brown eyes avoided his. Well, after all, she *was* working.

"Yes, of course. Who did it, do you know?"

Elena ceased her work and stared at him. "No!"

"Well, too bad, because I want to find out. I'm a private detective."

"I know you are. We all know that." She began working again. He saw the bun of her brown hair, in a net on the back of her head, moving, nodding, as her face was turned downwards. After a moment, Archie said, "And of course, as it happened in here, that night, it may have been one of the staff."

Elena nodded once more, causing Archie some surprise at her failure to react more strongly. He took time to think, and then asked her, "Of course, no staff was supposed to be here at the time, so we don't know who could have come in here with Mr. Trout, do we?"

She shook her head no, and finished buffing his nails, quietly. He stood.

"Thank you, Elena. I hope to see you another time. Good work."

Henry wasn't there, but Markie took the payment at the front counter.

So, what had he, now? Not much. Should he try to squeeze more info from his pal Ralph? Police never like to reveal more than they have to, even if the listener is a former Navy shipmate.

Archie had to question the husband, but where was he? What address? What last name, even? Manifestly, Ralph was the only hope. But what approach? Ralph would see through guile, and anyhow, Archie was all for honesty these days. So, whether Ralph liked it or not, Archie had to admit he was working on the case, without a client, for the heck of it, and that Ralph knew things Archie didn't.

He went to bed after a little exercise and a shower and a couple of beers and a small cigar and a local news program.

The next day when he drove to see the sergeant, after calling for an appointment, there appeared to be a problem: he noticed, out of long habit of being watchful, that he was being followed. Or at any rate, he was fairly certain. It took a few turns, evasively, to lose the tail. Not a "pro," he discerned. An amateur. Who could it be? Elena's husband? The barbershop had his phone number and address, so perhaps Elena had been able to procure it. But this car Archie thought had been tailing him was a classy vehicle. Would her husband have such as it?

Well, Archie had lost him, and proceeded to the police station, and to Sergeant Ralph Carpenter's office inside the building.

The large black man sat at his desk with a sour look on his face.

"Hello, Ralph," Archie said.

Ralph grunted. "Suppose you need more info. What?"

Archie sat in a chair facing the sergeant. He smiled. 'I wish I had more info to give you in exchange for that which I need –"

"Yeah," Ralph remarked briefly.

They stared at each other.

"But...considering our long history, our friendship, I will make but one request, although it's a big one."

"Yeah," Ralph repeated.

"You see, I know about the affair between the barber and the wife of the suspect."

"Suspect?"

"Sure. What's his name? I want his name and address to finish my investigation, and then –"

Ralph guffawed. "Funny. Who's your client, Archie?"

"Well, see, that's hard to tell. But between us, there isn't any client. Just me."

"You? Why?"

"I...like that barbershop, I want to clear this all up. I guess the husband of the manicurist did it, but what evidence is there? I doubt you have any. I want to find some."

"Okay. How?"

"By talking to the husband, whatever his name is, and, well, following a lead or two."

"What leads?"

"Uh...." Archie hesitated.

"Yeah. *We* have *one* lead." Ralph looked at a paper on his desk. "Confidential," he murmured. "I'm taking a risk showing you this, but what the hell." He tossed the paper in Archie's direction. Archie smiled, picked it up, and read it.

"Ah-ha!" He glanced from the paper to Ralph. "A love note?"

"So it seems."

But it was a lot more than a love note. It was a threat. It said, "I can kill you both, Les and you. But if you will give him up for me, no one has to die. Love, Fred." It was handwritten. Archie whistled.

"What do you think?" he asked Ralph.

"Incriminating, except...."

"No shit," Archie responded. "Fred's plan went badly awry. Incriminating for Les, for sure. Is he the manicurist's husband?"

Ralph nodded. "But...he has a good alibi." Archie whistled once more. "That complicates things."

Ralph said nothing, so in a minute or two Archie stood, thanked him and turned to go, saying, "I suppose you aren't going to tell me where that note came from."

"Not for now, buddy."

He didn't notice any tail as he went to the market, purchased a few items, and cruised to his apartment.

That was a relief. He hated being followed, since it usually didn't turn out well.

He ate, he drank whiskey, he watched the news and an old Hawaiian Eye episode on a cable channel showing old TV programs, and calculated another visit to Leo's Barber Shop was in order – to question the boss, again. Armed with that note's alarming words, Archie felt that the boss *had* to have further knowledge. Maybe. It was worth trying.

Yet before that, an idea hit him: what if the boss was in love with Elena? It had happened that way before, an employee caught in a boss's crosshairs. But if her heart was set on Fred, Henry might have been unable to control his jealousy, his anger, and shot Fred in what sometimes is referred to as "a crime of passion." And Henry *might* have an expensive car, and tailed Archie.

He'd have to find out, the sooner the better. But how? Can't just ask Henry.

So, Archie parked at a safe distance from the barbershop lot, and watched and waited. Finally, the boss exited the front, and walked to a BMW sedan, it seemed to Archie, deactivated its alarm, and climbed in. That was the car.

Bingo.

But to follow him? Why not?

It was uneventful, a tail job to a man's house. Archie, knowing how to do it, was sure he wasn't spotted.

So he waited, watching the place after Henry entered from the carport, and began to be bored.

If Henry had plugged Fred, he wouldn't very easily reveal it. He'd be concealing it from the police, at least, careful about his every move.

Nevertheless, Archie waited more than an hour, and drove off, tossing it all to the wind, disgruntled. Let the police handle it. They had men, weapons, and money. Archie had nothing except himself, really.

In the morning, he told Ralph all he knew, and washed his hands of it. Except for one more talk he wanted to have with Elena. If that led somewhere, great. If not, he could look for a job, perhaps at a news organization. He'd had experience with that in the past, gathering news and providing copy. All he'd need was a good reference.

The morning vanished as he adjusted his carburetor, determined to approach Elena without lying. He also cleaned the windshield and even scuffed up his nails on the sidewalk before driving to the shop.

He waved his fingernails at Henry as he strolled to the manicurist's station. "Emergency," he intoned. "Elena available?" It seemed the best approach.

The boss opened his mouth but said nothing, and nodded his head.

Archie walked to the rear, entered the alcove, and spotted both Faye and Elena, sitting with apparently not much to do.

"Hello!" he announced to them. "Your fine work has been assailed," he said to Elena, showing her. "I cleaned them a little, but...." he said. "I was fixing my car."

Her eyes were wide. "Oh!" She took his hands, examining the fingernails. "Shocking," she laughed. "Sit down." Faye was watching, and laughed, too.

So far so good, Archie told himself.

He got his nails done, but not the answer to his big question. Both women were mute as to who had loved Elena enough to kill for her.

Not that he'd expected a lot. His experience as a P.I. taught him that finding important information from guilty, or even non-guilty, persons surrounding a murder, did not come easily. A better detective might have found out more, but those two were refusing to comply, in his opinion.

Archie's parting shot, "You won't tell me, but wait until the cops have at you," produced a gasp from Faye and a scowl from Elena. Not quite the desired effect, but close enough.

He paid at the counter and slipped out.

Something was nagging him, certainly. Why were they hiding *anything*? What could it matter? Knowledge of wrong-doing? Likely, he figured, but not necessarily. Those women may think what he'd asked was none of his business (true) and letting him in on it wasn't called for.

Had one of them killed Fred Trout? Possibly, but not likely. Did they know who did? Possibly.

But Archie had no idea what to do next. He'd have to wait and see what the police came up with. He spent the day trying to think of a plan, but not being a genius, he wasn't able to.

Time passed; he made up a short resume to provide to prospective news organization firms. Most news copy was online these days, but still a paper or two published dailies. What would they ask of him? He dug out a few copies of his work from years ago, printed it up, and put it with the resume. All set...but a reference or two were needed. He came up with them using email, reaching out to people he'd dealt with in the past.

But the murder at the barbershop still bothered him. It wouldn't be long before he contacted Ralph again, to ask for an update. Archie couldn't wait very much longer. His nerves were on edge. A murderer was out there, needing to be apprehended. Perhaps he could help with that.

Those women! The boss! The other barbers! The husband! An unrelated intruder! Who did it?

Finally, he contacted Ralph by phone, and learned nothing new. So the stalemate persisted.

He had an idea, though. A bizarre idea. To pursue it meant breaking the law, something P.I.s occasionally did. But Archie saw no alternative. He could lose his license if caught. But...so what?

He began by digging out the tool kit he had acquired – tricky items to nullify alarm systems and open locks – even sophisticated locks. The days of simple lockpicks were long over.

He needed an address – Les and Elena's house or apartment. He practically was forced to beg Ralph for it. He said he wanted to make a surveillance – he told Ralph he suspected them. Archie had to promise he'd avoid any confrontation, if possible. Ralph, reluctant, gave him the Foremans' address. That was the name he *finally* provided Archie with. But their address was the main issue.

Parking nearby, that afternoon, Archie realized how exposed he'd be outside the residence. But what choice had he? The small place was brick and wood, with a tiny lawn in the front. Windows spied down on him as he approached. Well, if spotted, so be it. A detective leads a life of danger – no avoiding it.

He went up the walk to the door, and rang the bell. No one came to open up. He rang again, waited. Nothing.

He looked up at the windows, he looked around the surrounding area. No one in sight. He took a deep breath, and pulled out the package of tools and keys from his pocket. Of course, Archie told himself, he'd been trained to go to the back door and knock, or ring, just in case, and enter that way. A lock may be simpler, for the back way. But he shrugged it off. What the hell, he thought. If someone was watching, what possible good would it do to go to the rear entrance? If he was arousing suspicion, that would simply add to it. So he made a professional attempt to open the front lock after assuring himself no burglar alarm was in evidence. But, surprisingly, he heard a latch clicking behind the door, and only just pulled his lock tool away when the door opened. He nearly dropped his kit on the ground.

A man stood just beyond the threshold, a questioning look on his face.

"Yes?"

"Oh, uh, pardon me. I rang – did you hear it?"

"Yes. Who are you?" He was wearing a robe, with his hand in one pocket.

"Archie Gordon, private investigator. I was trying to get out my case, to leave..." he gestured at his pocket, casually with his toolkit, as though he'd been digging around in his pocket, merely attempting to find a card. The man nodded impatiently.

"But what the hell do you want?"

Archie smiled. "That's a question I'd just as soon not answer until I know who *you* are."

"Fair enough, Gordon. I live here. Les Foreman."

"Ah-ha! Might I see I.D.?"

"No. Take my word for it."

"Umm, okay. I wanted to question you as to the murder at Leo's Barber Shop a few weeks ago."

That took him down a peg. "Is it any of your business?"

"Somewhat. I can't reveal the name of my client, though."

"In that case, goodbye." Foreman closed the door, and Archie was relieved.

Now what? He hadn't forgotten that Henry had followed him, but what good was that? If Les killed Fred, maybe Henry knew it, but why tail Archie? What good would that do, unless Henry was part of it, and worried, worried directly about Archie stirring it all up.

And what would Les do now?

Anyway, the threatening note from Fred was the key, but Ralph wouldn't divulge much. Had they searched Les's house? Archie had an idea, and called Ralph. It took awhile to reach him but he did, and asked if the police had found a gun at Les's. No good; Ralph refused to say.

"Okay, but here's an idea. Get a warrant, and search Henry's place – look for the murder gun. Well, any gun, and have it tested."

"You suspect him?" Ralph questioned.

"I do." He told him why.

The warrant was issued – a judge friendly to the police had been approached – and Ralph himself, with others, had served it and conducted the search of Henry's abode. No gun was found, but something else: a note from Fred, to Henry, accusing him of being an obstacle to Fred's love for Elena. It was stashed below a loose plank in a large desk drawer.

Archie got the information with a warning not to reveal it to anyone – especially Ralph's superiors. Ralph would inform *them* himself.

Fine. Now it seemed Henry might have shot Fred Trout, who he didn't want to have Elena. Wow, thought Archie. How will it ever be proven?

In his apartment once again, he went over it all in his mind. Suspects, but no proof. He drank beer and puzzled, as the T.V. droned.

Have to trip Henry in some way. Or make Elena talk. Good luck with that, he told himself.

If he goes to the barbershop *again*, he will have no cover. He needed no haircut and he couldn't fake that fingernail scam again. Or could he? Maybe it was worth a try. They'd all think it was weird, but so? At least he'd be inside and have opportunity to question Henry and maybe Elena, if she wasn't occupied. Shoddy, though. Archie's former boss would frown on it. Yet he couldn't come up with a better scheme.

He looked in the mirror. Possibly he might require a cut, if he had a specific purpose, say, like going to a wedding or an invitation to the White House. Ha!

Archie let that wait until morning. Coffee and a fresher view of it might be productive. And of course, he didn't want to lie.

So the next day, he arrived ar the barbershop with a plan in mind. No lying. He waved at Henry again, and pointed to the manicurist's station. He smiled, too, and Henry only shrugged, so Archie proceeded to the alcove, hoping for the best.

Faye was working – a middle-aged, well-dressed woman sat with her. That is, well-dressed as far as he could tell – she wore a green smock, like Faye did. Elena was missing, so Archie took a seat, smiling at Faye, wondering how his plan would work, now. Instead of telling Elena he had been to the house and had spoken to her husband, and after her expected shocked reaction, asking her did she believe he had killed Trout, Archie would need to question Faye. But what? Did she believe Foreman had killed Trout?

And on top of it, he had no reservation for a manicure. What was he thinking? Some detective. Archie was attracted to Faye's blonde hair but slipped off to see the boss about an appointment. He waited while Henry attended to a customer, and then joked, "If I keep coming so often, I'll ask for a discount," chuckling so Henry wouldn't mistake the comment as being serious.

"Okay now," Henry began. "Which of the girls?"

"Either one, today if at all possible."

Henry studied the schedule on the computer screen, and finally said, "Today with Faye at four. How's that?"

"Fine. Thanks. Elena off?"

"Out on personal business."

"Oh."

Henry entered information to the appointment schedule, and nodded when done.

"Hope her husband isn't the problem. I met him once and he's a grouch."

Henry stared at Archie. "A mean fellow? I know."

"Has he been here hassling her?"

"Yep."

"Jealous?"

Henry was quiet, but his eyes were intense.

"For instance, jealous of you," Archie offered.

"Me? Hell, no. Who are you kidding?"

"Not attracted to Elena? Apparently Fred was…"

"None of your business, Mr. Gordon. Is it?"

"I suppose not. See you later."

He had planned to return at four, but first Archie needed to ask Ralph, his good friend Ralph, a question, that later caused him to cancel the appointment.

But first, it took so much time to reach Ralph that Archie despaired of *ever* getting him, but he did.

"Buddy, please tell me what you think about that note from Fred to Henry. I'm begging."

"Oh? You have something? I ought not say, I ought to bring you in and –"

"Oh my God. I have a suspicion. I'll spill it; methinks the boss shot Fred Trout. And if you will say you think that, and that Elena is involved, you will clinch it."

"Really?"

"Because she *knows*, she even helped Henry with the murder. She could testify to it if you get her immunity."

"You say so?"

"I hope so."

There was a slight pause, and Ralph said, "Yes, I do think the same."

"Good. Now hear this: the note to Henry got to Elena, somehow, and Foreman, of course. She had to show it to him. And why not? But Elena decided she'd rather have

Henry, the boss with a future, than Foreman, a cold fish. What his future is, you know better than I. But anyway, she gave the note back to Henry, and said he had to do *something*, an appeal which might have included a smile and a kiss. Henry fell for it. Or he asked her would she stick with him, and she said emphatically, 'Yes, darling,' and so...."

"He killed Fred?"

"Sure. To blame it on Les Foreman!"

"Hmmmm..." Ralph slowly murmured.

Wrapping it up was not easy, but police departments are good at that. District attorneys are good at that, too. And Ralph took most of the credit. Henry was convicted, Elena got probation due to her witness testimony against Henry. Archie? He found a job with a newspaper, meeting deadlines once more, and felt happy.

Printed in Great Britain
by Amazon